Fast Facts About Dogs

Fast Facts About
GOLDEN RETRIEVERS

by Marcie Aboff

PEBBLE
a capstone imprint

Pebble Emerge is published by Pebble, an imprint of Capstone.
1710 Roe Crest Drive
North Mankato, Minnesota 56003
www.capstonepub.com

Copyright © 2021 by Capstone. All rights reserved. No part of this publication may be reproduced in whole or in part, or stored in a retrieval system, or transmitted in any form or by any means, electronic, mechanical, photocopying, recording, or otherwise, without written permission of the publisher.

Library of Congress Cataloging-in-Publication Data is available on the Library of Congress website.
ISBN 978-1-9771-2452-4 (library binding)
ISBN 978-1-9771-2495-1 (eBook PDF)

Summary: Calling all golden retriever fans! Ever wondered about a golden retriever's personality? Want to find out the best way to care for this type of dog? Kids will learn all about golden retrievers with fun facts, beautiful photos, and an activity.

Image Credits
Capstone Press/Karon Dubke, 20; Getty Images/Bettmann, 19; iStockphoto: andresr, 4, Andyworks, 11, FatCamera, 12; Shutterstock: all_about_people, 16, Antoni Gravante, cover (left), Ekaterina43, backcover, ESB Professional, 15, Hollydogs, 5, Linn Currie, 6, 9, Monkey Business Images, 13, New Africa, cover, Orientgold, 7, Photo_mt, 17

Artistic elements: Shutterstock: Anbel, illustratioz

Editorial Credits
Editor: Megan Peterson; Designer: Sarah Bennett; Media Researcher: Kelly Garvin; Production Specialist: Tori Abraham

All internet sites appearing in back matter were available and accurate when this book was sent to press.

Table of Contents

A Golden Dog 4

Golden History 8

Lively Goldens 10

Keeping Goldens Healthy 14

Caring for Goldens 16

Fun Facts About Golden Retrievers 18

Make a Sock Bottle Dog Toy 20

Glossary 22

Read More 23

Internet Sites 23

Index 24

Words in **bold** are in the glossary.

A Golden Dog

Golden retrievers are friendly dogs. They like to spend time with children and adults. They play well with other pets too. Goldens are smart and gentle.

Golden retrievers like to please. They love playing fetch with their owners. Throw a ball to a golden. The dog will bring it back to you. Toss a dog toy into the water. Watch the golden swim for it!

Golden retrievers have thick golden fur. Their fur can be wavy or straight. They have a **double coat**. The topcoat keeps them dry. The bottom coat keeps them warm.

Goldens are large dogs. They weigh 55 to 75 pounds (25 to 34 kilograms). They stand 21 to 24 inches (53 to 61 centimeters) tall. A golden is about the same size as a Labrador retriever.

Golden History

The first golden retrievers were **bred** in Scotland in the 1800s. They helped bring back **game** for hunters. They searched for game on land and in water. Goldens came to the United States in the early 1900s. Today they are one of the most **popular** dogs.

Lively Goldens

Goldens are lively dogs that love to swim. They are great at dock diving. In this sport, the dog waits on a dock. A dog toy is tossed into the water. The golden runs down the dock. She jumps into the water to grab the toy. Goldens can jump far!

Golden retrievers like to help people. They make great **guide dogs**. Guide dogs wear a vest and harness. A blind person holds the dog's harness. Goldens help them get around safely.

12

Goldens also help sick people. They visit hospitals. People like petting goldens. Goldens help people feel peaceful and happy. They have a lot of love to give.

Keeping Goldens Healthy

Most golden retrievers are healthy. They should visit a **veterinarian** once a year. The vet will check the dog's heart, ears, and teeth. She will also check the dog's eyes and lungs. Sometimes older goldens have hip or elbow pain. Some have problems with their heart and eyes. Goldens live for 10 to 12 years.

Caring for Goldens

Goldens have lots of **energy**. They need daily **exercise**. Goldens like hiking and swimming. They are happy playing fetch. Golden puppies should be trained early. Untrained goldens can get into trouble!

Golden retrievers shed a lot. Their fur should be brushed daily. Bathe them once a month. Goldens love to eat. Sometimes they eat too much! Feed them only at mealtime.

Fun Facts About Golden Retrievers

- Goldens keep their playful puppy ways even as adults.

- Goldens can have light to dark golden fur.

- A golden retriever starred on the TV show *Full House*.

- Goldens are the third-most popular dog in the United States.

- Former president Gerald Ford had a pet golden retriever named Liberty.

Make a Sock Bottle Dog Toy

What You Need:

- empty plastic water bottle
- an old sock

What You Do:

1. Place the plastic bottle into the sock. Push it all the way to the end of the sock.

2. Tie the open end of the sock into a knot. Ask an adult if you need help tying the knot.

3. Throw the sock toy! Watch your golden bring it back.

Glossary

breed (BREED)—to mate and raise a certain kind of animal

double coat (DUH-buhl KOHT)—a coat that is thick and soft close to the skin and covered with lighter, silky fur on the surface

energy (EH-nuhr-jee)—the strength to do active things without getting tired

exercise (EK-suhr-syz)—a physical activity done in order to stay healthy and fit

game (GAME)—wild animals hunted for food or sport

guide dog (GUYD DAHG)—a dog that is specially trained to lead people who are blind

popular (POP-yuh-lur)—liked or enjoyed by many people

veterinarian (vet-ur-uh-NAYR-ee-uhn)—a doctor trained to take care of animals

Read More

Bozzo, Linda. *I Like Golden Retrievers!* New York: Enslow Publishing, 2017.

Gray, Susan H., and Maria Koran. *Golden Retrievers.* New York: AV2 by Weigl, 2018.

Klukow, Mary Ellen. *Golden Retrievers.* Mankato, MN: Amicus/Amicus Ink, 2020.

Internet Sites

American Kennel Club: Golden Retriever
https://www.akc.org/dog-breeds/golden-retriever/

Animal Planet
http://www.animalplanet.com/breed-selector/dog-breeds/sporting/golden-retriever.html

Ducksters
https://www.ducksters.com/animals/golden_retriever.php

Index

body parts, 6, 14

care, 14, 16–17

dock diving, 10

exercise, 10, 16

feeding, 17
fur, 6, 17, 18

guide dogs, 12

history, 8
hunting, 8

size, 7
swimming, 5, 10, 16

training, 16